CASTLE INTRIGUE

Paul Stewart
Illustrated by Jane Gedye

Editor: Phil Roxbee Cox
Assistant Editor: Michelle Bates
Series Editor: Gaby Waters

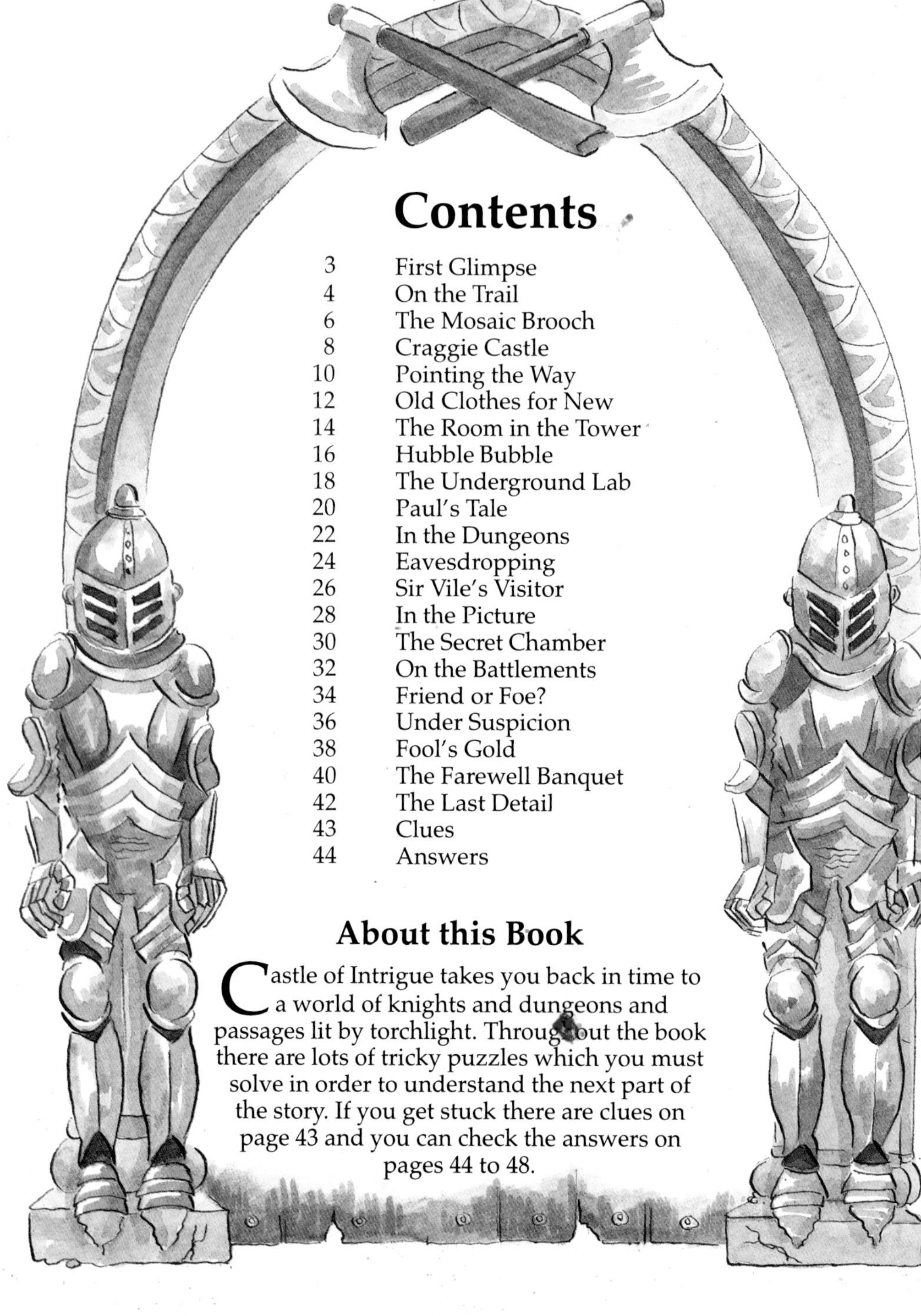

Contents

About this Book

Castle of Intrigue takes you back in time to a world of knights and dungeons and passages lit by torchlight. Throughout the book there are lots of tricky puzzles which you must solve in order to understand the next part of the story. If you get stuck there are clues on page 43 and you can check the answers on pages 44 to 48.

First Glimpse

One April, Sally Bolt was sent to stay with her Aunt Bertha. This was the first time she had been away without her parents. And she was looking forward to it.

Sally had never met her aunt before, but she had heard a great deal about her. Bertha Bolt was fanatical about local history. She had lived in the same cottage all her life. Although it was right out in the middle of nowhere, she wouldn't move anywhere else.

The nearest town was called Stormycliff. It was a dismal place by the sea, famous far and wide for its terrible weather.

Today was no exception. As the train neared the station, heavy storm clouds gathered overhead.

Sally peered through the window excitedly. Suddenly, a dazzling flash of lightning lit up the ruins of an amazing castle perched on top of a rocky hill.

On the Trail

Aunt Bertha met Sally at the station. One hour and a hair-raising car ride later, they arrived at her ramshackle cottage. Within minutes, they were sitting down to homemade flapjacks and rosehip tea.

Aunt Bertha asked Sally if she would help her pick out a new potato peeler in town. Sally couldn't think of anything worse.

"Actually, I thought I'd go and take a look at that castle on the hill," she said politely.

"In this rain?" her aunt said. "You'll catch your death of cold! I've got a much better idea. You can go tomorrow if the weather is better. In the meantime, I'll dig out everything I have on Craggie Castle, and you can look through it all while I'm out."

"If I must," Sally sighed. As well as a guide book, maps, brochures and photos, there was also a battered ancient-looking, leather-bound book.

Aunt Bertha noticed Sally's surprise at the author's name on the spine. "He must have been a distant relative of ours," she explained. "It's been in the family for generations. Must dash, bye for now!"

"See you later," said Sally opening the guide book at the first page. The more she read, the more interested she became. It was full of curious details about the history of Craggie Castle. She could hardly wait to explore the castle itself.

The Mosaic Brooch

The next day was sunny. Eager to get started, Sally was ready to leave before Aunt Bertha had time to make the breakfast.

Her backpack was bulging with everything Sally thought she might need: guide book, lucky rubber spider, tape recorder, maps, and an enormous packed lunch.

Waving goodbye, Sally set off up the steep hill toward the huge fortress of Craggie Castle. Some time later, she heard running water up ahead, and soon came to a set of stepping stones.

On the far side of the river, the ground was squelchy wet from the previous day's rain. Sally watched the mud ooze around the sides of her boots with each step.

Suddenly, she noticed something glinting on the ground just in front of her. Unable to stop in time, she trod on it.

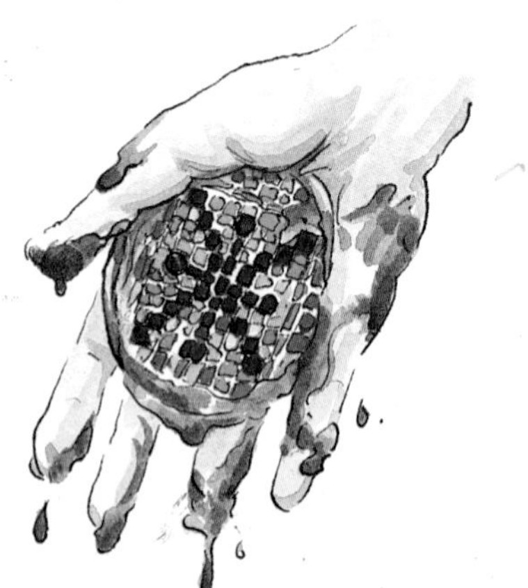

"Bother!" Sally muttered, as the object vanished. She knelt down and rooted around in the mud. "Here it is," she cried a few moments later.

In the palm of her hand was a tarnished silver brooch with an inlaid mosaic pattern. It looked old. It even felt old!

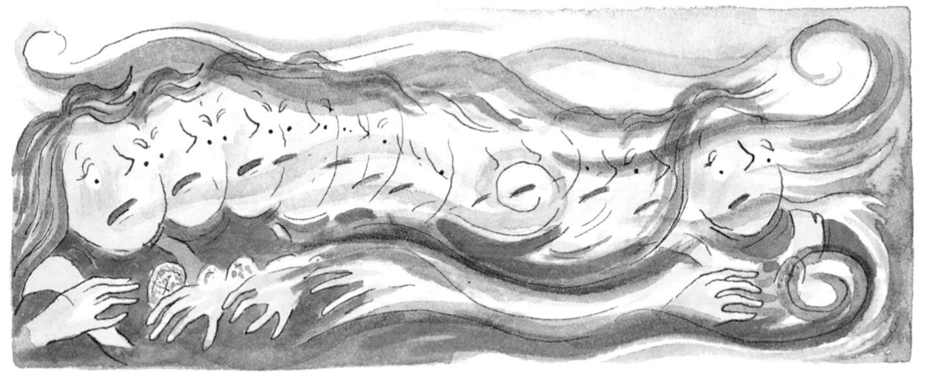

As she pinned the brooch to her sweatshirt, Sally felt dizzy, as if she was falling. The sun abruptly disappeared and she found herself cloaked in a thick, choking fog. It was like nothing she had ever experienced before. She was unable to see, and soon hopelessly lost.

Sally wandered aimlessly until she came to an old, broken signpost. Pulling a map from her pocket she realized that she should still be able to discover which way to go.

Which path leads to the castle?

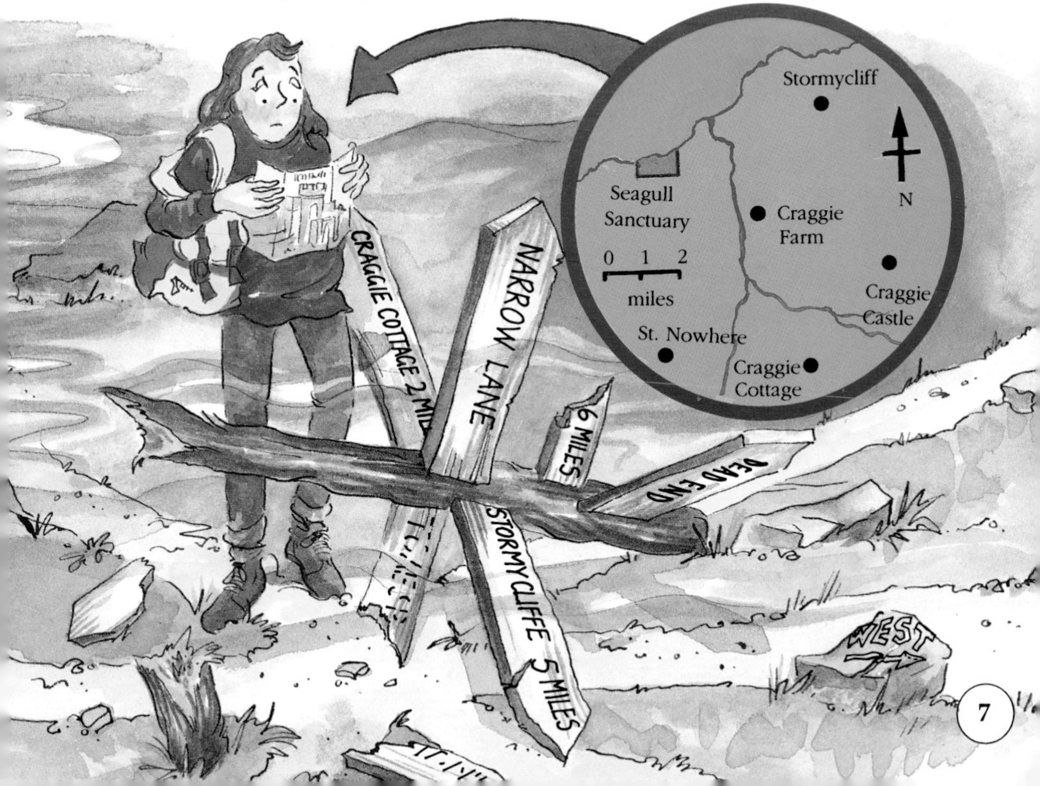

Craggie Castle

Sally puffed her way up the hill. The fog slowly cleared and the sun beat down hotter than ever. Ahead of her, the castle gleamed in the sunlight. For some reason, it looked less of a ruin than Sally had remembered. But then again, she had only caught a hurried glimpse of it the day before, lit up by the lightning as the train had sped past.

By the time she reached the drawbridge Sally was feeling very uneasy. Something was wrong! For a start, there were goats dotted around the place. And why were there so many people about so early in the morning? She could hear the low babble of voices coming from inside the castle walls. If they were tourists, where were the tour buses?

In the courtyard, Sally stood open-mouthed. The place was packed with people dressed in funny clothes. Of course, they must be making a film! But where were the cameras and lights, and who was the director? It all looked and sounded so medieval. Sally wrinkled up her nose. It even *smelled* medieval.
You've had your bacon!
I've heard Sir Vile's planning to tax water next.
There you are.
You've got to look your best for tomorrow's Midsummer's Day Joust.
ARRGH!
Bewildered, Sally looked around. It made no sense. Either she was dreaming, or she had somehow gone back in time. Sally was in the medieval past of the castle! Her thoughts were interrupted by a boy hurrying toward her. She recognized him at once. But where from? And what was different about him?
Do you know?

Pointing the Way

Stranger still, the boy seemed to think he knew Sally and even wanted something from her. Sally's head was spinning. What was going on? "How did you know my name?" she asked.

"The brooch, of course," Paul replied. "This latest message has your name in it and mentions the brooch," he said, thrusting a piece of parchment with a poem on it into her hand. Sally read it quickly.

The time has come for us to fight,
To put the wicked wrongs to right.
To rouse the sleeping rebel faction
And put our plotting into action.
Sally forth and find the silver brooch,
Match it to the window you must then approach.
There, look behind the coat which is not warm,
Nor keeps you dry in rain or wild storm.
Despite the bearskins, one, two, three,
Above an emerald fleur-de-lys.

"Sally forth isn't a name," she laughed, pointing at the poem. "It's a . . ."

"Have you had a message too?" Paul interrupted.

"No," she said. "But I think I know where this message is telling you to go to find the next one!"

"*Us* to go," Paul smiled.

What has Sally seen?

Old Clothes for New

They were just about to set off for the window when Sally noticed a couple of guards staring at her.

"You need new clothes, and quickly," said Paul. "Sir Vile rules his people with a rod of iron, and woe betide anyone who steps out of line." Paul knew, only too well, how dangerous it was for anyone at Craggie Castle to stand out.

Mim's Medieval Modes

Page boy
Vassal
Guard
Falconer
Jester
Juggler
Musician
Groom

He led Sally to *Mim's Medieval Modes* and handed her two silver coins. "Buy yourself something from here so that you'll fit in with the rest of us," he said.

Sally tried on a rough brown tunic and immediately started scratching.

Paul laughed. "Do you have any hidden talents?" he asked pointing to a brightly painted board. "Falconers wear more comfortable costumes. Are you good with birds?"

Sally shook her head. "No, but I can play the guitar," she said.

"The what?" asked Paul. Sally strummed on an imaginary guitar.

"Aha, something like a lute," said Paul. "In that case, there is no problem. You'll find everything you need over there."

Can you find all the things that Sally needs?

The Room in the Tower

Sally paid for the clothes, pocketed the change and hurried off with Paul. A moment later, they stood at the heavy oak door which led up to the room with the cross-shaped window where the message was hidden.

They pushed it open, went in and climbed a dark, spiral staircase. Half way up, they heard voices just above them. They froze. The guards on the battlement – Hugo Zare and Fred O'Foe – were changing watch.

"What news, Hugo?" asked Fred."How went the night watch?"

"F . . . fearful," came the reply. "I saw the ghost again."

"Dreamed it in your sleep, more like. I ought to report you."

"No!" he pleaded. "Anything but that! You know Sir Vile's punishment for sleeping on duty!"

When the guards had left, Paul and Sally continued cautiously up the stairs. Sally wondered what kind of a man Sir Vile was to cause such terror. When they reached the top they found themselves in a shadowy chamber, full of jousting equipment. Sally and Paul looked around in utter confusion.

The next message could be anywhere. Suddenly, in a flash of inspiration, Sally remembered the 'coat' in the poem Paul had shown her. It could only mean one thing. She glanced up and smiled. "I know where it is!" she announced.

Where is the message?

Hubble Bubble

Sure enough, behind the shield, they found the note. It looked faded, as though it had been written years ago. It appeared to be a few lines from a play but could it be a kind of password?

"Allspice! The cook!" Paul exclaimed. "So he's in on it too!" He set off to the kitchens with a puzzled Sally following close behind. She wondered exactly what the cook could be 'in on'.

I had almost given up hope that anyone would ever come.

The soup looks good!

What? Oh, er, Methinks it needs more salt.

Her confusion grew when they reached the kitchen. Paul repeated the words from the message, and the cook responded, with a look of both fear and relief on his face.

Reaching up into a jar of flour, he retrieved a small bag. He handed it to them with shaking fingers and steered them to the back door. "Go now!" he whispered urgently. "If I were you . . . " he added, but then fell silent.

Outside, they examined the contents of the bag. There was a small phial of green liquid, a torn piece of a letter and a large oatmeal biscuit. Baked into one side were the words, 'DIVIDE AND SHARE.'

Paul broke the biscuit in half and out popped a message. He laid it down on the ground and they examined it closely. It was a jumble of letters in a language neither of them had ever seen before. It must be written in code.

Then Sally remembered Allspice's curious parting words: "*If I were you*". Perhaps they had more than one meaning? Sally smiled triumphantly. Of course, that was it. She'd have the message deciphered in no time.

Can you decipher the message?

Kszz rcbs! gc tof gc uccr. Hvs
dvwoz qcbhowbg ufsazcqy. Wh
kwzz gsbr hvcgs kvc eiott wh
wbhc o vsorm gzssd. Hvs zshhsf
wg hvs twfgh dcfhwcb ct am
twboz wbghfiqhwcbg. Sbgifs
hvoh ozz hvs dwsqsg mci twbr
gvozz aohqv, zsgh gcascbs gvcizr
ohhsadh hfsoqvsfm. Odczcuwsg
tcf ozz hvwg wbhfwuis, pih
hcbuisg rc kou obr kozzg vojs
sofg. Hcc aiqv ybckzsrus wg o
robusfcig hvwbu tcf cbs ozcbs.
Gssy ms bck hvs gsqcbr vwrrsb
dzchhsf. Asfuobgsf. Vwg asggous
kwzz pfwbu mci cbs ghsd
qzcgsf hc as. Obr uccr ziqy!
(Hvs qcrskcfr wg uczr)

The Underground Lab

Sally pointed at a name in the decoded message. "Who's Merganser?" she asked. "He sounds like a heavy metal band!"

"Castle talk has it that he's an alchemist, hidden away by Sir Vile. His job is to turn metal, light or heavy, into gold," Paul explained.

"Hidden where?" Sally asked.

"I've heard it said that to work, he needs a room *'shut away from the moon and sun, with water beneath that does not run'*."

Sally examined her layout of the castle. Only one room fitted the bill. It was an underground chamber in the middle of the castle, with its own private well. They hurried to it.

Stepping over a snoozing guard, they entered the candle-lit chamber. A man, who looked like a wizard, was muttering some mumbo-jumbo under his breath. Paul gave the password.

"Gold?" Merganser said sadly. "Would that it were, I . . . Oh, I see!" he said, as it struck him who the two visitors must be. "So the rebellion is finally under way after all these years of waiting."

As Merganser was removing a bag from its hiding place, there was a sudden knock at the door. It was the castle guards. Sally and Paul froze to the spot, both petrified that they were about to be arrested. They looked around for somewhere to hide.

"No, it's me they want, not you," said Merganser. "I got the job because I said I could turn lead into gold to pay for Sir Vile's wicked life of gambling and gluttony. Sadly, I cannot! If the plot . . . er . . . I mean *when* the plot succeeds, do remember me!"

Paul and Sally slipped out by a back door, only to find themselves in an unfamiliar set of dimly lit corridors.

"I don't know this part of the castle so well," Paul confessed.

For the second time, Sally pulled the castle layout from her pocket. She scrutinized the plans carefully. It appeared that only one door led to safety.

Which door should they choose?

Paul's Tale

They lifted the bar on the door and opened it. Paul and Sally cautiously entered the pitch black room. Suddenly, the door slammed shut. To their horror, they heard the bar drop back into place. They were trapped.

"Great!" said Sally. "Now we've locked ourselves in!"

"Only because you misread the map," Paul snapped back.

"Don't blame me," shouted Sally angrily. "It's the map that was wrong."

"I'm sorry," he muttered.

"Fair enough, but will you tell me exactly what is going on?" Sally said crossly.

"All right," came Paul's voice from the darkness, and he began to tell his story . . .

My parents were Sir Bevidere the Benign and Lady Gwendolyn. When I was two, my father went to fight for the king in faraway lands.

Two years after that, word came that he had died upon the battlefield. As proof, the messenger returned with my father's precious sword, *Veritas*.

The bearer of these bad tidings was the rogue, Sir Vile the Vile. He took the castle for himself, and raised his flag above the battlements.

My grieving mother was imprisoned, but managed to have me smuggled out. I later heard that she had died of a broken heart.

I grew up in the court of Sir Boris the Bold, my uncle. He was a good man who vowed to free the land of so wicked a tyrant.

Twice my uncle tried, and failed, to re-capture the castle. To be successful, any attack must come from within.

Sir Vile ruled with an iron fist. He introduced crippling taxes where none had existed before and showed no mercy to the downtrodden peasants.

Meanwhile, he lived a life of luxury, drunkenness and gambling. His pet dogs grew fatter while the poor people on his land had barely enough to eat.

And so an intricate plot was hatched, though I don't know who was behind it. I returned to Craggie Castle, disguised as a page.

I studied hard to become a knight. As well as jousting, I can read *and* write. But I grew impatient, waiting for the uprising to begin.

And now it has. One message leads to another message, and to another fellow plotter. Until I reach the final message . . .

. . . which shall be a signal that the battle is to commence. We must not fail. The people have suffered enough.

"Wow!" said Sally. "That's some story, and now I'm actually a part of it. I'll do everything I can to help you."

Coming from the future, Sally wished she could tell Paul how things would turn out. Unfortunately, the poem that might have held the answer was missing its end. All she could do was hope.

"The first thing we have to do is to find a way out of here," said Paul. "And that could take an absolute age."

"But time is the one thing we don't have," said Sally. "I think I know precisely *when* the uprising is due to start."

When is the uprising supposed to take place?

In the Dungeons

If Sally was right about the timing of the uprising there was no time to lose.

She looked around and sighed. Now that her eyes had grown accustomed to the dark, it was clear just how bad their situation was.

"It looks like a dungeon," Sally muttered miserably.

"That's because it is a dungeon," came a voice out of the shadows.

Horrified to find that Paul's tale had been overheard by someone else, Paul and Sally spun around. What if he decided to betray them? "Who's there?" Paul demanded suspiciously.

"I, Ludolf,' came the reply.

And there in the corner, chained to the wall, was someone dressed just like Sally. "Sir Vile, the vile rogue, suspects that something is afoot,"said the court lute player. "The guards are rounding up everyone suspected of treachery to stamp out any rebellion before it has even begun."

Paul and Sally looked around frantically for some way out. Then Sally spotted something that gave her an idea. Just as they were about to put her plan into action, Ludolf spoke.

"There is one thing I was told to say to you. If, when out of here you need a key, then '*the key you must seek is the key of G*'."

"Thank you," said Sally, doubtfully. "We won't forget you."

How do they plan to escape from the dungeon?

Eavesdropping

Free from their prison at last, they suddenly remembered the bag that the alchemist, Merganser, had given them.

"But I have to serve at the high table now, to avoid suspicion and punishment," Paul groaned, brushing down his tunic.

Tomorrow's tournament starts at twelve noon.

Ay, and the King is to attend.

They say a ghost is plotting the overthrow of the present Lord!

Where is the oubliette exactly?

On no account is that renegade Sir Boris the Bold to be allowed in.

All the invited knights are here save Sir Plus the Excessive. He is coming tomorrow afternoon.

Taxes are to go up again.

Allspice and Ludolf have been arrested, and Merganser is under suspicion.

As Paul moved unnoticed around the Great Hall, waiting on Sir Vile and his guests, he listened to what was being said. All at once, he overheard something which filled him with panic.

Meanwhile Sally had found a second fragment of the letter in the bag, along with a piece of spiralled horn and yet another message.

What does the message say?

Sir Vile's Visitor

Later, as the knights and their ladies retired to bed, Sally and Paul found a quiet corner where they could talk about what they had learned.

"We've got to see Magnolia the painter," Sally explained, and was shocked by Paul's reaction.

"Oh no!" he groaned, "I heard someone say that she is about to be arrested."

Perhaps she would have had time to conceal the message somewhere. They would have to go to her studio once everyone had settled down for the night.

"Why don't you get some sleep while we're waiting," said Paul. "I'll wake you when it's time to make our move."

Sally didn't argue. She was exhausted. Unfortunately, so was Paul. Fifteen minutes later, they were *both* fast asleep.

They were rudely awakened by the sound of screaming. Looking up, they saw guards racing to Sir Vile's bedchamber. Sally and Paul crept over to the door and peeked in. Sir Vile was sitting bolt upright in an enormous bed. He was shaking and looked as though he'd seen a ghost.

Then something caught Sir Vile's attention. Something he found even more terrifying than a ghost. Sally and Paul ducked back out of sight. It wouldn't do to be caught snooping around his bedroom.

Just as Sally was leaving, she noticed two things of importance. Not only did she see what had so upset Sir Vile, but she also learned something about the so-called ghost.

What has she seen?

In the Picture

While the castle was still in uproar, Sally and Paul made their way to Magnolia's room. The door was ajar. Paul pushed it open.

"We're already too late," Sally groaned. "How are we going to find the next clue now?"

They entered the studio and looked around. All at once, Sally noticed a pile of broken pieces of slate lying under the table. They had clearly been kicked out of sight deliberately. She crouched down. The slate was covered in charcoal sketches of tiny shields.

"Have a look at this," she called to Paul. "I think it could be important. Help me to put them back together again."

Bit by bit, they reassembled the jigsaw of broken pieces. Sally and Paul became more and more puzzled. What did it all mean?

There were two familiar words at the top of the slate, and lots of little shields and letters all over it. But what were they for? Sally hadn't a clue.

"That's it!" exclaimed Paul. "It's telling us to look at Sir Vile's portrait over there. I'd know that wicked scoundrel anywhere. The message must be hidden in the shields around the edges."

Sally nodded. "With Allspice, Merganser and Ludolf under arrest, she must have known that the guards would come for her too. That's why she hid the message."

"Then let's get it deciphered and wipe the slate clean," said Paul. "The guards could come back at any moment."

What do the shields spell out?

The Secret Chamber

Following their latest instructions, they turned down yet another long corridor. "Are you sure that we're going the right way?" asked Sally.

"Of course I'm sure," said Paul. "In fact, here we are," he exclaimed with glee, a triumphant smile spreading right across his face.

Set in the wall was the torch they had been looking for. As Paul turned it to the left, Sally found the square stone and pressed it.

A secret door opened to reveal a secret chamber. Inside, they soon found the casket. But it was locked. "We need a key," sighed Paul. They began to search high and low.

They had almost given up hope. Paul was about to smash open the box, when Sally suddenly cried out. "Wait. Ludolf talked about a key and I know where it is!"

She was right. "It fits the casket perfectly!" She turned the lock, opened the lid and they peered inside. It was empty apart from a letter and a couple of cards. Paul laid them out on the table.

I am sorry not to meet you in person, Paul, but so many of our number have been arrested that my plans have had to be revised. I wrote the letter, and split it into three parts, in case I was captured and could not give you my instructions directly. Magnolia was to have given you the third part. Now this is not possible. But have faith. The usurper will be usurped! I have now had this final part of the letter hidden on the north battlements. You will find it in a crack in the mortar nine strides from the tower steps. Go there now, but beware of Sir Vile's guards. They are under orders to arrest anyone acting suspiciously.

TRUST YE.

TRUST YE NOT.

Sally sighed. The secret bedchamber was indeed where the head plotter had been hiding out, but he, or she, had already gone. "This paper chase is never-ending," she said. "Now what do we do?"

"Exactly what the letter says," Paul said grimly. "Come on." As they left the room, Sally had a final look around. Then, she noticed something.

"Of course," she said. But Paul put his finger to his lips just as she was about to explain what she had seen. There was someone coming!

Thankfully, the guard Paul had heard passed by without noticing the secret door. Paul headed off toward the north battlements. Sally followed behind.

How had Sally known where to find the key?

On the Battlements

Up on the battlements, Sally stopped and stared around her. She gasped in amazement. It was so beautiful. The full moon shone, white and dazzling, while the stars – millions and millions of them – had never seemed brighter.

"Come on," said Paul sharply.

Sally hurried over to join him at the tower steps. With heads down, they began counting their way along the parapet. Four paces later, they walked slapbang into an angry guard.

"Who goes there?" he said in a gruff voice.

"I'm Paul the pageboy and this is . . ." Paul faltered. Who could he say she was? "Sally the songmaker!"

"Yes," Sally joined in. "I come here for inspiration. *The moon, in June is a balloon,*" she began singing.

"That's enough of that noise," said the guard. "Be off with you now, before I clap you in irons!"

When they were sure that the guard had gone, Paul and Sally returned for the hidden message. And there it was, sticking out from a crack in the wall.

Finally they had the entire letter. In a shadowy alcove, they spread out the three pieces on the floor.

What does the letter say?

Friend or Foe?

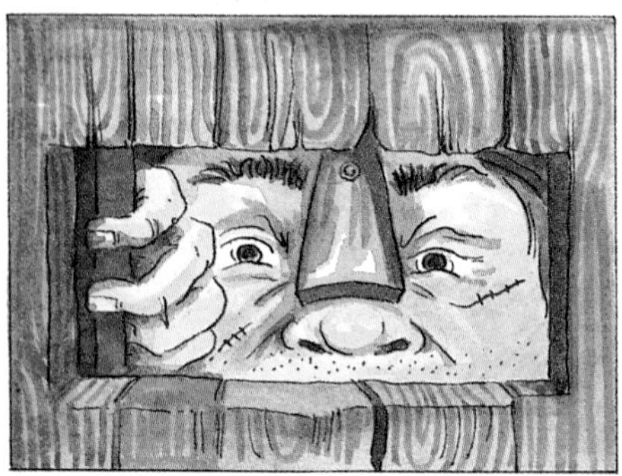

Paul and Sally hurried to the gatehouse as the letter had instructed. When they arrived at the door, Sally handed Paul the phial of gremlock.

"I hope this stuff works," said Paul pouring the gremlock into the jug of cider.

"It's the so-called unicorn horn I'm worried about," said Sally. "Unicorns don't exist!"

"Of course they exist!" exclaimed Paul. "Everyone knows that." Sally smiled, but kept quiet. Paul knocked on the door, and a small wooden window opened.

"Oh, it's you Paul," came a voice. "And with refreshments!"

The bolts slid open and Paul disappeared into the gatehouse. While Sally waited for his return, she looked across to the Midsummer's Day joust.

Despite her head being full of the sound of thundering hooves, Sally couldn't stop thinking about the task at hand. Then she heard the portcullis being raised behind her, and spun around to see who was entering the castle.

As the knights on horseback clattered over the drawbridge, Sally stared nervously. Were they really Sir Plus the Excessive and his men, or Sir Boris and his soldiers come to save them?

Then Sally saw something which made her smile with relief.

What has Sally noticed?

Under Suspicion

When Paul did not return, Sally grew worried. She pushed the door and went inside. The guard at the door was asleep. Another lay on the stairs. When she reached the wheel-room, Sally saw that all the guards were sleeping soundly.

To her dismay, Paul was slumped by the far wall. She prodded him. He was very groggy, but awake. Just.

Slowly, he came to his senses. When his head had cleared, he told Sally what had happened.

"I only poured out drinks for the guards, but they said that I had to join in the toast too. Then, to my horror, I realized I'd lost the horn.

"I took the merest sip, but that was enough to turn my body to lead. Then, I heard a voice. *'May fortune smile upon the good!'* it cried.

"I dragged myself to the window, and there outside was my uncle. With my last ounce of strength I raised the portcullis. Then I fell back to sleep."

"We've got to get going," said Sally urgently. "The letter told us to pass on Sir Boris the Bold's message to Ludolf."

Paul nodded. "If he's been set free, I know where to find him."

They ran to the kitchen garden. Paul had noticed that the lute player was in there when they had fled Allspice's kitchen.

They saw a familiar figure sitting on a low wall, strumming his lute.

"We meet again," said Ludolf. "Have you a message for me?" "Indeed," Paul nodded. "But first, let us drink to your new found freedom," he said, and passed Ludolf the jug of cider.

"To freedom," Ludolf announced as he raised the jug to his lips. Before Sally even realized what was going on, Ludolf swigged from the jug . . . and promptly fell asleep.

"Are you mad?" she cried.

Why has Paul sent Ludolf to sleep?

Fool's Gold

The imposter was now out of the way, but Paul and Sally still had a problem. They had to deliver Sir Boris's message to the real Ludolf and he must still be imprisoned. They dashed to the newly repaired window of the dungeon and peered inside.

"Ludolf," Paul whispered. "Are you alone?"

"No," came the reply. "I have the traitor Merganser with me. He knew that my part in the plot to return this castle to its rightful heir was to sing one of two messages."

"Forgive me," wailed Merganser.

Ludolf paused for breath. "The first message means that the attack on the castle will be abandoned. The second means everyone must rise up as planned."

"And he betrayed you to Sir Vile?" said Sally.

"When he failed to make gold, he had to come up with something to save his own neck. So he traded information," he said. "But still ended up down here."

"Sir Boris said *'May fortune smile upon the good,'* whatever that means," said Paul.

"Oh no!" said Ludolf. "Those were the words I was to sing for the uprising to go ahead."

"All is not lost," said Paul. "I can sing the words in your place."

"Sadly not," Ludolf sighed. "All those awaiting the signal have been instructed to listen out for my voice, and mine alone. While I'm safely locked up down here, the uprising will never happen. Never!"

"Nonsense," said Sally, realizing for the first time why someone from the twentieth century had been needed. She pulled her tape recorder from her bag and told Ludolf to sing his call to arms when she gave the signal.

Ludolf looked unsure. "Trust me," said Sally.

Without understanding why, Ludolf sang his piece as instructed. His voice was certainly unique. It was awful! Once he had finished, Sally played back the tape.

At that moment, the door flew open and a guard appeared, ordering Merganser to follow him. Paul and Ludolf gasped, realizing how foolish they had been talking in front of the traitor. What if he betrayed them a second time? Only Sally remained unconcerned.

What has she noticed?

The Farewell Banquet

Paul and Sally hurried to the Great Hall, which had been decked out with banners and pennants for the banquet.

While the guests found their seats, Paul and Sally took up their positions. With her hood concealing her face, Sally pressed play on the tape recorder, and began strumming on her lute.

When the wailing reached the ears of Sir Vile he almost choked on his food. "You told me he was locked up!" he screamed, Ludolf's voice echoing around the hall. "Silence him at once!"

But the tape recorder would not be silenced. Even as one of the guards lunged at Sally, the song continued to the end.

At once, the Great Hall erupted into feverish activity. Sir Boris and his men drew their swords and, with the loyal conspirators, swiftly overpowered Sir Vile's guards.

But what of Sir Vile himself? When calm had finally been restored, the rebels saw to their horror that the wicked tyrant had escaped. Seeing the door to his bed chamber ajar, the guards raced in to arrest him . . . but the room was empty.

Suddenly, Sally remembered the tell-tale marks she had seen on the tapestries. Sir Vile must have noticed them too. "I think I know where we'll find him," she said.

Where does she think Sir Vile is?

The Last Detail

With Sir Vile's men under arrest and loyal guards on their way to the Secret Chamber to seize Sir Vile himself, everyone burst into excited conversation.

Just then, a regal figure, with sword raised aloft, appeared in the doorway. The assembled gathering turned and gasped.

And so it was over. Sir Vile was tossed into the dungeons. All those he had imprisoned were set free. And *Veritas* was returned to its rightful owner, Paul the Page, who was knighted there and then.

Paul's grandmother, Lady Gloriana, turned to Sally. "It was my messages which guided you, but your sharp wits and clever tricks saved the day."

"Thank you Sally Forth," cried Paul.

Sally laughed. "Actually, it's Sally Bolt."

"Bold, you say?" Paul said. "So you're bold by name as well as by nature. You must be related to Sir Boris!"

"Your time is done or, should I say, yet to come, Sally," Lady Gloriana interrupted. "It's time to return the brooch."

Reluctantly, Sally unpinned the brooch and handed it over. She blinked. In an instant, she found herself looking at the crumbling ruin of Craggie Castle. She was back in her old clothes.

Sticking her hands in her pockets, her fingers closed around two strange coins. Puzzled, she pulled them out and looked at them. It was the change from the costume stall, now aged with time. Sally smiled. She *had* been there.

Clues

Pages 4-5

Look carefully at all of the information here. It could prove to be vital later.

Pages 6-7

Try to locate Sally's exact position on the map. Then you should be able to discover which direction she should go to reach Craggie Castle. The stone pointing west is a vital clue.

Pages 8-9

A picture on pages 4-5 might help you here.

Pages 10-11

Try reading the poem again. Does the pattern around one of the windows look familiar?

Pages 12-13

A lute player is a musician.

Pages 14-15

Perhaps they should look for something with a particular *coat*-of-arms on it?

Pages 16-17

'If I were you' is the key to this code. Think of letters of the alphabet to crack it.

Pages 18-19

Something on page 5 might be useful here.

Pages 20-21

Look back to the poem on page 5. Have you spotted anything else along the way that might help you too?

Pages 22-23

They need to reach the window, but how? Remember, most things are too heavy to move, or too broken to stand on.

Pages 24-25

Can you see a sequence of letters running through this message that shouldn't be there?

Pages 26-27

Is something missing? And ghosts don't leave chalky handprints – do they?

Pages 28-29

The slate holds the key.

Pages 30-31

The answer lies in music!

Pages 32-33

Try tracing the pieces of paper and fitting them together.

Pages 34-35

Something on page 4 could be very useful. Then just use your eyes.

Pages 36-37

Look closely at the message on page 33 and think back to what you saw on page 18.

Pages 38-39

The cards on page 31 could be useful. Study them closely.

Pages 40-41

Look carefully at the tapestries on pages 27 and 30. They have a similiar design which could be more than just a pretty pattern.

Answers

Pages 6-7

Sally knows that Craggie Cottage is two miles behind her and Stormycliff five ahead of her, so she can pinpoint her position on the map. She realizes that she is directly east of Craggie Castle. As the only milestone points west, Sally knows that she must take the path that goes in the opposite direction. It is shown here.

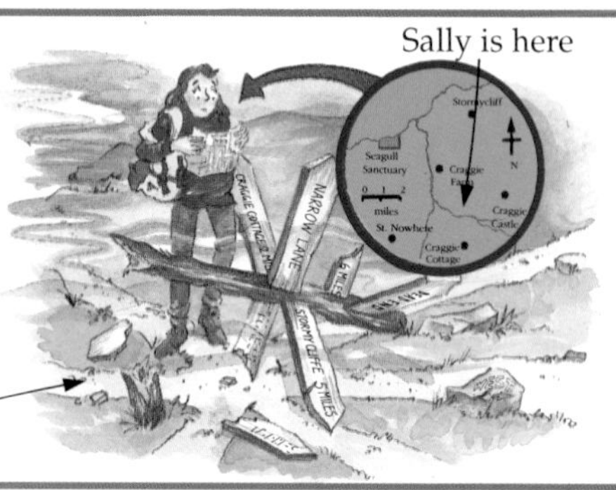

Pages 8-9

Sally recognizes the boy from a picture in the guidebook on page 5, only now he is wearing a tunic with a yellow stripe rather than a red cross.

Pages 10-11

Sally has seen the window that is mentioned in the message. It is circled here. She recognizes it because it is an exact match to the pattern on the silver brooch.

Pages 12-13

Sally looks at the board to discover what a lute player would need. As a lute player is a musician, she needs to buy the things shown here.

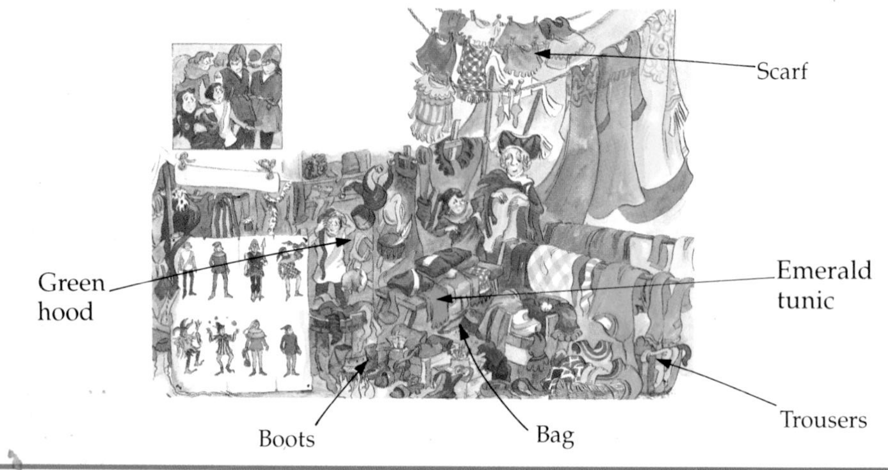

Pages 14-15

The next message is on the back of the shield circled here.

The 'coat' in the message is a coat-of-arms. The 'bearskins, one, two, three' are the three bears. At the bottom is the 'emerald fleur-de-lys'. (There is a picture of a fleur-de-lys on page 4).

Pages 16-17

Sally realizes the significance of the words 'If I were you'. The message has been written in code so that when the letter u appears it is actually the letter i, v is really the letter j and w is really k and so on. When decoded the message reads:

> Well done! So far, so good. The phial contains gremlock. It will send those who quaff it into a heady sleep. The letter is the first portion of my final instructions. Ensure that all the pieces you find shall match, lest someone should attempt treachery. Apologies for all this intrigue, but tongues do wag and walls have ears. Too much knowledge is a dangerous thing for one alone. Seek ye now the second hidden plotter, Merganser. His message will bring you one step closer to me. And good luck!
> (The codeword is GOLD)

Pages 18-19

Using the plan of the castle on page 5 and studying the layout of the doors in the corridor, Paul and Sally realize that they are in the area shown here.
According to this, there is only one door that can lead them to safety, marked here with a cross. Unfortunately, it leads them straight into the dungeons because the map is wrong. The plan shows how Craggie Castle is today. The historian who drew the map made the mistake of thinking that's how part of the basement was in medieval times.

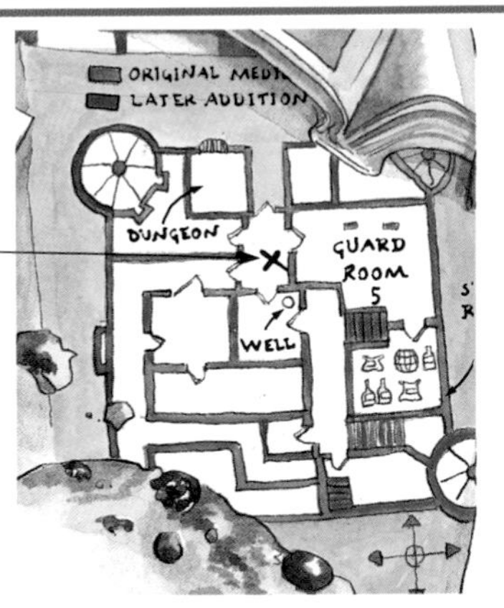

Pages 20-21

The uprising should take place tomorrow. Sally knows this from two pieces of information. In the poem on page 5 it says that the uprising took place on the day of the Midsummer Joust. She knows that the Midsummer Joust is to be held the following day because on pages 8-9, the groom in charge of Charger wants him to look his best for the Midsummer Day Joust the next day.

Pages 22-23

The window with the missing bar is the only way out. But how can Sally and Paul reach it? The rack is too heavy to be pushed and, as the trestle table has broken legs, they wouldn't be able to stand on it. They cannot use the ladder as it is broken, and the swinging cage is padlocked into place. They must take one of these pikes and push it sideways through both of the rings below the window to make a platform, as shown here. They must then pull themselves up onto this 'pike platform' and then stand on it. From there, they will be able to reach the window and pull themselves up and through the gap.

Pages 24-25

The letters in this message are grouped in fours rather than in their actual words, then an extra letter is added to the beginning of each group. (The first of these letters is A, the second B and so on). To decode the message, remove the extra letters, then add punctuation and spaces between the words. This is the message:

CONGRATULATIONS. YOU ARE NOW ONE STEP NEARER TO ME. THE UNICORN HORN IS FOR YOUR PROTECTION. PLACED IN FOOD OR DRINK, IT DRIVES AWAY ANY POISON THEREIN, THAT YOU MAY SATE YOUR APPETITE OR QUENCH YOUR THIRST IN SAFETY. SEEK YE NOW MAGNOLIA, THE PAINTER OF PORTRAITS. SHE SHALL SHOW YOU HOW TO FIND ME!!

Pages 26-27

Sally and Sir Vile have both noticed that the sword, *Veritas*, has been removed from the wall. But Sally has *also* noticed a white chalky hand print on the edge of the tapestry. This is proof that the ghost isn't really a ghost at all, but must be a living person dressed up for the part!

Pages 28-29

Paul and Sally put the broken pieces of the slate back together and realize that it is the key to a code. Each shield represents a different letter of the alphabet. This is shown here.

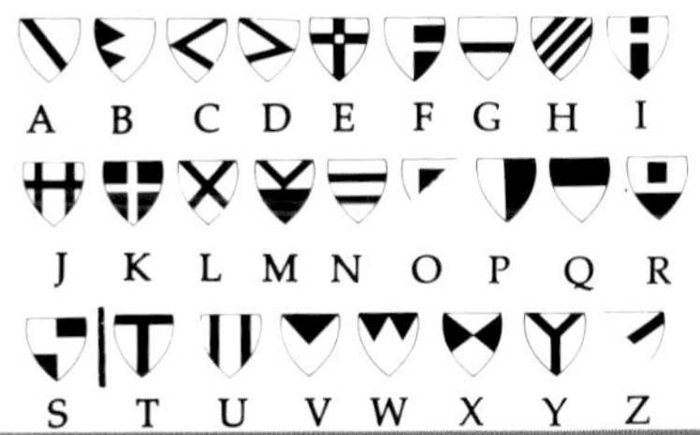

Although the shields for the letters O and Z are not complete, there is enough information to enable Paul and Sally to decode the message in the shields around the portrait of Sir Vile. Once decoded and with punctuation added it reads:

MY SECRET CHAMBER LIES BETWEEN LIBRARY AND CLASSROOM. PRESS SMALLEST SQUARE AND TILT TORCH LEFT. COME NOW. OPEN CASKET.

Pages 30-31

The key of G is actually a musical term. Sally therefore looks at the embroidered music on the tapestry and finds the key next to the treble clef.

Pages 32-33

The three pieces of paper do fit together, revealing the following message:

Paul, If you have reached this stage, you will have brought new hope to those brave men and women who have been waiting for this moment. They have led normal castle lives, knowing that one day they would be required to give a message to someone. That someone is you. Your asking for their messages was a signal for them to prepare for the overthrow of the cruel Sir Vile. They are ready, know their places, and await your final move. Our clever intrigue is about to bear fruit. Go to the drawbridge at a quarter before noon on Midsummer's Day. Take cider, laced with Allspice's gremlock, to the guards on the gate, that they may toast the commencement of the tournament, and so dream of victory! Stir your own cup with the horn that *you* will not sleep. Sir Boris, your uncle, is to ambush Sir Plus the Excessive on the way. He will arrive wearing the red uniform of Sir Plus and his men. Lower the drawbridge and let him in. If the ambush goes wrong, DO NOT allow Sir Plus to enter! Next, you must get word to the castle guards who remain loyal to the memory of Sir Bedivere, that Craggie Castle has been breached successfully. Do this as follows. When Sir Boris passes through the gates, listen to his cry. Pass on his words to Ludolf the left-handed lute player. He will then broadcast the good news through a ballad at this evening's revelries. Without this coded message, no one will act. If all goes to plan, not a drop of blood will be spilt. The people have suffered enough already!

Pages 34-35

Sally sees two things that make her realize that the ambush has been successful. She recognizes Sir Boris's horse, from a picture on page 4. It has a black front half, and a white back half. From page 4, Sally also knows that Sir Boris and his men wear blue. The tiny flash of blue under the red costumes confirms that the men are wearing the uniform of Sir Boris.

Pages 36-37

When Paul and Sally see Ludolf on page 18, he is playing his lute left-handedly and Gloriana specifically tells them on page 33 to give the message to the *left-handed* lute player.

The person Paul and Sally meet in the garden is playing the lute with his right-hand and is clearly an imposter.

Pages 38-39

Sally has noticed that the guard has his belt fastened with the tongue pointing to his right. Sally remembers the two pictures of guards they found in the casket in the secret chamber (on page 31). One showed one of Sir Vile's guards with his belt fastened the proper way, its tongue pointing left. The other showed a conspirator with his belt fastened the other way. This is a clever secret signal to other conspirators telling them which guards are on their side. Sally has spotted that this is a friendly guard, only pretending to carry out Sir Vile's orders.

Pages 40-41

Sally remembers two patterns that she has seen stitched into two different tapestries: one in Sir Vile's bedchamber (on page 27), and one in the secret chamber (on page 30). They are in fact maps showing a secret passage connecting them. At first glance, these maps – cleverly disguised as patterns – look identical. If you look closer, you will see the crosses are in different places. These crosses show which room you are in. The so-called "ghost" must have disappeared from Sir Vile's chamber through the secret connecting passage. If, as Sally guesses, Sir Vile has also made this deduction, he has probably tried to escape to the secret chamber himself.

This edition first published in 2005 by Usborne Publishing Ltd., 83-85 Saffron Hill, London, EC1N 8RT. www.usborne.com
First published in America in 1994. UE. Printed in China.